CHURCH GIRL LOST

By

Laadie Ohh

For every woman who's ever lost herself trying to be what the world demanded, may you find your way home.

Prologue ~ The Weight of Sunday Morning

The air in southern Georgia always carried a kind of heaviness, the kind that seemed to rest on your skin and your heart at the same time. Even the mornings felt full, swollen with humidity and memory. On Sundays, that heaviness deepened until it became something holy, or at least that's what everyone said.

For **Laneshia Jonelle Stanson**, Sundays had once meant something close to sacred. As a girl, she used to measure time by church bells and altar calls. Now, at forty-three, she measured it by deadlines and exhaustion. But the memory of those mornings never left her. The thick scent of honeysuckle, the rusted screen door creaking in rhythm with her mother's commands, and the sound of gospel hymns floating down the road like ghosts that refused to die.

This Sunday morning began like so many others had: quiet but expectant. The world outside her apartment window hummed with a low summer heat that had not yet broken, the kind that pressed through glass and walls alike. A ceiling fan spun lazily above her bed, slicing the silence into patient, predictable pieces.

She sat at the edge of the mattress, elbows on her knees, coffee cooling on the nightstand beside her. The clock read 9:27 a.m. In another life, she'd be halfway through service by now. Maybe clapping along with the choir, maybe forcing a smile at Sister Mae's pointed remarks about single women "waiting on the Lord." But these days, church felt like another kind of performance. One she no longer had the strength to perfect.

Her phone buzzed once. A text from her coworker:
You joining the team brunch?

She stared at the screen, thumb hovering, then set it face-down. The thought of small talk over mimosas exhausted her more than staying in bed ever could.

Instead, she rose and walked toward the window. Outside, the city was already alive. Atlanta sunlight spilled across brick and pavement, catching on the glass of passing cars and the mirrored surfaces of high-rise offices. Somewhere in the distance, a church bell still tolled.

It wasn't the same as home. The bell sounded metallic, rushed, without the deep warmth of the one she'd grown up hearing. But it was enough to pull her backward.

Back to the red dirt roads of **Waycross, Georgia**. Where the air shimmered with heat and the only thing louder than the cicadas was her mama's voice calling her inside.

Laneshia closed her eyes and let the memory bloom.

In Waycross, Sunday mornings began before sunrise. Her mama, **Ruth Ann Stanson**, believed the Lord didn't bless those who showed up halfway. By six, the house was alive with movement. Biscuits baking, the iron hissing and gospel radio turned up loud enough to wake the dead.

"Jonelle!" her mother's voice would echo through the hallway. "Don't make me come in there and find you still lyin' down when the Lord done got up!"

Laneshia would groan softly. The thin cotton sheets sticking to her skin. The fan in her room was too small to battle Georgia heat, and her pillow always smelled faintly of starch and sweat.

"I'm up, Mama," she'd call back, though she rarely meant it.

Her brother, **Terrence**, would already be dressed. Tie hanging loosely around his neck and shoes shining like mirrors. He'd grin that grin. The one that always got him forgiven before he even needed to be. “Come on, slowpoke,” he’d tease, tapping her shoulder as he passed.

Their mother would appear a moment later, her church hat pinned high, lipstick precise as a prayer. “You best be grateful to the Lord for another breath in your body,” she’d say, half blessing, half warning.

Laneshia had learned early that gratitude and silence were often the same thing.

By the time they piled into the family’s old Buick, the sun would already be climbing, the road steaming from last night’s rain. Her mama’s perfume, White Diamonds, filled the car like incense, and every breath carried the scent of both holiness and suffocation.

At the white church down the road, the choir would already be warming up. The organ spilling laughter and lament into the air. Inside, the sanctuary was always too hot! The windows cracked just enough for a breeze that never came. Still, people sang. They sang until the walls trembled. Until even the air seemed to shimmer with hope.

As a child, Laneshia loved those sounds. The clapping hands. The harmonies layered like call and response between heaven and earth. But even then, a small voice inside her whispered questions she wasn’t brave enough to ask:

Why did God’s house feel heavy when everyone said it should feel free?

The phone buzzed again, snapping her back to the present.
She ignored it.

Laneshia moved to the kitchen and poured herself another cup of coffee. Steam rose from the mug, fogging her glasses for a heartbeat before fading. She liked her apartment this way. Quiet. Organized. Hers. No cross on the wall, no family portraits staring down at her from decades past. Just clean lines, muted colors, and the hum of her own existence.

Still, there were days like this one when the past pressed against her like humidity. Thick, unrelenting, and impossible to ignore.

She carried it with her. Not as an open wound but as a scar that still ached before rain.

At work, she was “L. J. Stanson,” Senior Operations Manager for a growing tech firm. Efficient. Reliable. Measured. Her coworkers praised her ability to remain calm under pressure. To mediate conflict. Her quiet strength. None of them knew what it had cost her to become that woman.

Every Sunday she wondered whether that cost had been too high.

She leaned against the counter, tracing the rim of her mug with one finger.

She had once believed that salvation was a formula. Attend church, obey the rules, trust in God’s timing. But somewhere between the hymns, the betrayals, and the men who preached love but practiced control, the formula had fallen apart.

Now, she wasn’t sure if she believed in God at all or if she was simply afraid of what it meant to stop believing.

Outside, a siren wailed faintly, rising and fading like a distant lament.

Laneshia exhaled slowly, pressing a palm to the cool surface of the countertop. She was tired. Tired in the kind of way that sleep couldn’t fix.

Every week felt like the same cycle: work, eat, pretend, repeat. But Sundays carried a different weight. They reminded her of all the things she’d lost and all the things she still hadn’t found.

She thought of her mother’s voice again. Sharp. Commanding. Unyielding.

"You can't hide from the Lord, Jonelle. He sees you even when you think you're invisible."

Maybe that was what scared her most. The thought of being seen.

She picked up her coffee, walked back to the window, and whispered into the quiet room, "Then why didn't He see me back then?"

The words surprised her. Too soft to echo yet too honest to deny.

For a moment, the world seemed still. The hum of traffic below dimmed. The light shifted and the air felt heavier somehow. As if it recognized the question's weight.

The coffee had gone cold again by the time she sat down.

She didn't mind. The bitterness suited her mood — sharp, grounding, familiar. She stared at the mug as if answers might rise from the dark surface, the way her pastor used to say the Spirit rose in the believer's heart.

If that were true, she thought, then hers must have stayed buried.

She took a sip anyway, the taste pulling her back to a different Sunday, decades earlier — the one she'd never quite been able to forget.

It was **August 1994**, the summer before she left for college.

Waycross had been unforgiving that year. Heat rising off the ground in visible waves, cicadas screaming in the trees like a warning that no one understood. Her mother had been especially devout that summer, as though trying to bargain with God not to lose her daughter to the wider world.

Every Sunday felt like a test. A final one.

That morning, Laneshia woke before dawn, nerves already alive in her stomach. She lay in bed listening to the familiar house sounds: the groan of floorboards, the rattle of pots, the hum of gospel on the kitchen radio. The smell of butter and grits seeped under her door, mingled with the faint scent of Ivory soap from her mother's morning bath.

When she finally rose and dressed, she caught her reflection in the dresser mirror. A long face framed by tight curls, a touch of lipstick she'd stolen from her mother's drawer, and eyes that already looked too old for seventeen.

She tugged at the hem of her dress, white cotton, hand-pressed and tried to imagine herself anywhere else. College. The city. A life where people didn't know her by her mother's rules or her father's absence.

Downstairs, Ruth Ann stood at the stove, wearing her Sunday best: a lilac suit with satin trim and matching hat. Her posture was perfect. Back straight. Chin lifted. As though the Lord himself had stitched her spine with command.

"Morning, Mama."

Ruth Ann didn't look up from the skillet. "Morning, baby. You iron that dress right this time?"

"Yes, ma'am."

"Mm." A pause, heavy with disbelief. "Go on and get your brother. Tell him we leavin' in fifteen."

Terrence was still asleep, of course. He always had a way of testing their mother's patience without paying the price. Laneshia stood at his door for a moment, watching him snore under the hum of the ceiling fan.

She almost envied him. His ease, his charm, his ability to move through the world without carrying its judgment on his back.

"Terrence," she said softly. "Time to go."

He groaned but smiled, cracking one eye open. "We goin' to heaven today or just church?"

"Both, if Mama got anything to say about it."

He laughed. The kind of laugh that made it hard not to join in.

Downstairs, Ruth Ann's voice rose again, sharper this time. "Let's go! The Lord don't wait on the lazy!"

By the time they made it to **New Hope Missionary Baptist**, the parking lot was full. Men in suits and women in hats that looked like declarations of war against humility. The choir robes glowed gold under the morning sun.

Inside, the sanctuary was alive. The air shimmered with perfume, sweat, and expectation.

Laneshia found her seat beside her mother, clutching her Bible like a lifeline. She tried to listen as the preacher took the pulpit. His voice rising and falling like thunder. But her thoughts wandered to the acceptance letter folded neatly in her purse. To the map she'd drawn of the city she'd soon call home. To the freedom she'd dreamed of since she was old enough to spell it.

Then the sermon shifted.

The pastor's voice softened. His tone taking on that rhythm of pity disguised as care. "Now, we all know our young women be wanderin' these days," he said. Pacing slowly across the pulpit. "Think they too good for the Word once they get a taste of the world. But the devil got his hand in all that education, all that independence. We better pray our daughters don't forget who they belong to."

Laughter rippled through the congregation. Ruth Ann's hand landed firm on Laneshia's knee.

"Mm-hmm," her mother murmured, eyes fixed on the pastor. "You hear that?"

Laneshia's throat tightened.

"I hear it."

And she did. Louder than the organ. Louder than the Amen chorus. She heard every warning, every boundary, every promise of love that sounded more like ownership.

That was the moment something in her began to shift.

By the time the altar call came, she couldn't bring herself to stand. Not when her mother's eyes pressed into her like scripture. Not when the preacher called for "lost souls" to find their way home.

She sat frozen, hands clasped tight, the choir swelling around her:

🎶 *I once was lost, but now am found…* 🎶

But Laneshia didn't feel found. She felt trapped inside a song she hadn't chosen.

The memory faded like smoke as she sat now in her apartment, present-day Atlanta humming beyond the window.

That was the last Sunday she went to New Hope. A week later, she boarded a bus for Atlanta with two suitcases, $48, and a promise to herself that she'd never be the kind of woman who needed saving.

Life had since taught her that promises made in pain have a way of unraveling.

She thought she'd escaped the weight of Waycross. Its gossip. Its expectations. Its smallness. But sometimes she still caught herself praying under her breath without meaning to. Sometimes the old songs still found her in traffic or in the shower. Echoing like a ghost she hadn't yet learned how to bless or bury.

She took another sip of coffee. This time it didn't taste bitter. Just empty.

Her reflection in the window looked both familiar and foreign. A grown woman shaped by both rebellion and routine. Behind her eyes, that same question lingered. The one that had followed her from that hot August morning in 1994.

Can a girl raised on salvation ever really stop searching for it?

The day moved quietly around her.
Light crept across the kitchen floor, climbed the walls, and finally settled on the framed photograph above her desk. Her college graduation portrait. Edges yellowed from years of sun. She had almost forgotten it was there.

She walked over and brushed dust from the frame. In the picture, she was twenty-two. Chin lifted and eyes full of something that looked like certainty. The woman looking at it now could hardly recognize that expression.

Her phone buzzed again, a third time.
A new message. This one from her mother.

Morning, Jonelle. Remember service starts at 10 if you still thinking about coming. Pastor Holt say they got a new choir director.

Laneshia stared at the text until the words blurred. Ruth Ann never stopped inviting her, though she'd stopped expecting a yes long ago. The messages came every few months, like tides that refused to learn the shoreline had changed.

She typed a reply, then erased it. Typed again. Erased again.

Finally, she set the phone aside and turned back to the window.

Below, a man in a faded suit walked down the sidewalk carrying a Bible and a bouquet of plastic roses. He moved slowly, almost reverently, as if the street itself were a sanctuary. When he reached the corner, he bent down and tucked one of the roses into a crack in the concrete. Just one bright pink bloom standing against the gray.

Something in the gesture caught her.

It was small, almost foolish, but undeniably tender. A sermon in silence. The kind of faith that didn't need permission to exist.

Laneshia felt her throat tighten. She pressed her palm to the glass. The rose looked stubborn and alive, defiant even.

A thought rose unbidden: *Maybe belief doesn't disappear. Maybe it just waits for you to come back differently.*

The idea startled her. She stepped away from the window. Heart quickened by a feeling she hadn't named in years. not joy exactly, but possibility.

On the table sat an unopened envelope from her company's community-outreach division. She'd been asked to help organize a volunteer literacy program at a local shelter. A project she'd been avoiding. Now, she slid her thumb under the seal.

The letter inside was simple. Meeting details, contact numbers, a note that read, *Thank you for choosing to serve.*

She smiled faintly at the phrasing.
Maybe she wasn't choosing to serve. Maybe she was choosing to start.

Laneshia set the letter beside her mug and looked once more out the window. The man had gone, but the rose remained. Bright and improbable against the concrete.

She whispered a small, uncertain promise to herself:

I'll go. Not to church. Not yet. But somewhere that needs me.

Outside, a wind stirred, carrying the faint sound of a choir rehearsing in the distance. Voices rose and fell like memory itself. Half prayer, half song.

Laneshia closed her eyes. For the first time in a long while, she didn't turn away.

Chapter One ~ The Gospel of Good Intentions

The first thing Laneshia noticed about the community center was the smell. A strange mixture of floor wax, instant coffee, and something fried too long in old grease. It clung to the walls the same way sound did. Laughter, frustration, the squeak of sneakers, and the shuffle of papers.

She stood just inside the door, clutching her purse like armor, wondering how this fluorescent-lit building had come to feel more intimidating than any boardroom she'd ever entered. A poster beside her read: **"New Horizons Literacy Program: Every Word Matters."**

Every word.

Laneshia exhaled and brushed her hand over her neatly pressed blouse. Silently hoping she hadn't overdressed. Everyone around her moved with a kind of casual purpose. Jeans, cardigans, and sneakers. She looked like she'd come straight from a corporate meeting, and in a way, she had.

This had been a last-minute decision. Two weeks earlier, she'd passed the flyer on the bulletin board outside her office breakroom. At first, she'd walked by without a second glance. But that night, while she reheated leftovers in her small apartment, something about the words *"literacy outreach"* had returned to her. Like a soft knock on a closed door.

She hadn't prayed about it. Not really. She'd simply decided to show up.

"Baby, you lost or just shy?"

The voice startled her. Laneshia turned to see a petite older woman with silver hair pulled into a bun, wearing thick glasses that magnified her eyes just enough to make her look perpetually curious. She held a clipboard like it was an extension of herself.

“I’m uh, I’m here to volunteer,” Laneshia said, forcing a smile. “For the reading program.”

“Well, praise God for new hands.” The woman’s grin deepened, revealing a small gap between her front teeth. “Name’s Evelyn Holt. You must be Ms. Stanson, right? You emailed me last week.”

Laneshia blinked. “Yes, that’s me.”

Evelyn nodded approvingly. “Good. You’re already ahead of half my volunteers — most of ’em just show up and expect divine instruction.” She gestured toward the rows of folding tables. “We’re getting ready to start the evening session. I’ll pair you with a student in a minute. You ever tutored before?”

“Not officially,” Laneshia admitted. “But I love reading. And I used to help with Sunday school.”

Evelyn’s eyes softened. “That’s a start. Around here, all we really need is patience and compassion. Maybe a strong stomach for cheap coffee”, she said jokingly.

They both laughed, and some of the tension in Laneshia’s shoulders eased. She followed Evelyn into the main room, where clusters of volunteers and students were settling in. The sound of pages turning filled the air, along with the rhythmic cadence of words being sounded out loud.

At one table, a young woman with honey-brown skin and braids tied up in a bun was arguing with a toddler who refused to stay in his stroller. The little boy threw a toy across the table, hitting a workbook. The woman groaned, then caught Laneshia watching.

“Sorry,” she said, embarrassed. “He don’t like to sit still long.”

“No worries,” Laneshia replied, stepping closer. “He’s curious. That’s a good sign.”

The young woman smiled faintly. “That’s one way to put it. I’m Deja.”

"Laneshia."

Evelyn appeared beside them. "Perfect. Laneshia, this is one of my brightest students. Don't let her fool you. She acts like she doesn't care, but she's read half a GED workbook already."

Deja rolled her eyes. "Half's a stretch."

Evelyn winked. "Humility's good for the soul." She patted Laneshia's shoulder. "I'll let y'all get acquainted."

Laneshia took a seat across from Deja, adjusting her posture. "So, you've been coming here long?"

"Couple months," Deja said, flipping open her notebook. "Trying to get my GED before my son turns three. My mama says she'll help watch him, but…" She trailed off, shrugging. "Life be life-ing."

Laneshia chuckled softly. "Yeah. I get that."

She glanced at the workbook, noting the highlighted sections, the neat handwriting, the small doodles in the margins. Hearts, question marks, and stars. "You're doing great," she said, genuinely impressed.

Deja shrugged again but her lips curved upward. "You sound like Ms. Holt. You church folk always gotta encourage people."

Laneshia hesitated. "What makes you think I'm church folk?"

Deja smirked. "The way you talk. Like you trying not to cuss."

Laneshia laughed out loud, surprising herself. It was the first time in a while her laughter had come without effort.

They started the session, reading through a short story about a woman starting over after losing her job. Deja stumbled over a few words, but each time, she corrected herself with quiet determination. Between sentences, the little boy hummed softly, banging his toy against the table like percussion.

At one point, Deja paused mid-paragraph and said, "You ever start over, Ms. Laneshia?"

The question hit harder than it should have. Laneshia smiled faintly. "More times than I can count."

Deja nodded as if she understood something unspoken. "Yeah. Me too."

For the rest of the hour, they read and laughed. By the time the class ended, Deja had finished two full pages without help. She beamed with pride, holding her workbook like a trophy.

"You did great," Laneshia said sincerely.

"You sound surprised."

"I'm not. I just… love seeing somebody believe in themselves again."

Deja's eyes softened. "Maybe that's what I need. I need to believe I can be somebody again."

Before Laneshia could respond, a low, warm male voice drifted from the doorway:
"Deja, you need me to walk y'all to the bus stop?"

Laneshia turned. The man who'd spoken stood tall, late thirties maybe, wearing a faded denim jacket and an expression that was equal parts calm and kind. His presence seemed to pull attention naturally.

"Nah, I'm good, Mr. Malcolm," Deja said. "We'll be fine."

He nodded, then glanced at Laneshia. Their eyes met briefly. A flicker of curiosity. Recognition or something unnamed passing between them.

Evelyn called from across the room. "Malcolm! Come meet our new volunteer before you start packing up."

He walked over, extending his hand. "Malcolm Raines."

"Laneshia Stanson."

"Ah," he said, smiling. "Ms. Holt said we were getting new help tonight. Welcome to the circus."

She laughed. "It's a good kind of chaos."

"Only kind worth showing up for," he replied.

And for a moment, something unfamiliar stirred in her. A kind of lightness. Fragile but alive. She hadn't expected to feel anything like that here. Not surrounded by the smell of coffee and crayons.

When the evening ended, Laneshia stepped out into the cool night air, her heart both full and unsettled. The city buzzed around her. Indifferent and alive, but for once, she didn't feel invisible.

Maybe this was what faith looked like now. Not pews or hymns, but small moments of connection. Quiet acts of grace.

As she drove home, the streetlights blurred into golden streaks against the windshield. Somewhere deep in her chest, a new rhythm began to form.

A soft, uncertain gospel of her own making.

Malcolm Raines had learned to recognize the look of someone trying not to be seen.
He'd seen it in too many faces — in the shelter halls, in probation classes, in the late-night food pantry lines. That slight lowering of the shoulders, the way people folded in on themselves as though shrinking could make them invisible.

Laneshia Stanson had walked into the community center carrying that same posture. Polished…composed, but careful. The kind of woman who was used to being competent, in control, and absolutely terrified of being found fragile.

He respected that.

Most folks assumed his calm came from faith. Maybe once it had. But these days, it was habit. A kind of practiced serenity that came from watching enough pain to know that words rarely fixed anything. You just showed up. Listened. Tried not to make things worse.

He stacked chairs as the others cleaned up, his thoughts still circling back to her. She had laughed with Deja, not out of politeness, but with real joy. It had surprised him.

"Don't you dare be thinking about that woman already," Evelyn's voice called from behind him.

He turned, grinning. "I wasn't."

"You were," she said, dragging a box of supplies across the floor. "And I ain't judging. I'm just saying that one carries weight. You can see it in her eyes."

He paused, then nodded. "Yeah. I saw it."

“She’s here for a reason,” Evelyn continued, her tone softening. “Most people don’t volunteer for literacy programs unless they’re trying to rewrite something in themselves.”

He didn’t respond to that. Just kept stacking chairs, the metallic clang echoing in the empty room.

When the last table folded, he stood for a long moment, staring at the chalkboard. Someone had written a verse near the corner in messy cursive:
“Faith without works is dead.” — James 2:26

He’d used that scripture a hundred times in sermons before he’d left the pulpit. But tonight, it felt like something else entirely. Not obligation, but reminder.
He wondered, briefly, if Laneshia knew what kind of work faith required when it had been burned down to ash.

Laneshia lay awake later that night, the sound of the city leaking through her window. Sirens somewhere distant, the soft hum of tires on asphalt, a train whistling miles away.

She couldn’t stop replaying the evening in her mind. Deja’s quiet determination. Evelyn’s fierce humor. Malcolm’s voice…low… measured…carrying the kind of certainty she’d long abandoned.

She had almost told him she’d grown up in a church like his once. Almost said that she used to believe faith could fix anything until it didn’t. But instead, she’d just smiled. She wasn’t ready for that kind of honesty.

Her phone buzzed. A text from an unknown number.

“Glad you joined tonight. Folks like you make the room better. — M.R.”

She hesitated, staring at the screen. Then typed back:

“Thanks. It felt… good to be there.”

“Then come back next week. We can always use good hands.”

She didn’t reply immediately. Instead, she lay there in the half-dark, the phone warm in her hand, her thoughts tangled.

There was something disarming about his ease, his quiet confidence. But there was something else too. A flicker of warning. She’d learned long ago that charm could be a mask for manipulation. That spiritual men sometimes carried their own shadows.

Still, she smiled before setting the phone down.

It had been a long time since anyone had looked at her like she wasn’t invisible.

The following week, she returned.

The room looked the same. Folding chairs, scuffed floors, and mismatched posters, but it felt different. Deja waved her over, smiling shyly, and Malcolm was already there, talking to a small group of volunteers.

“Ms. Stanson,” he greeted her. “Back for more punishment?”

“Guess I’m a glutton for good causes,” she said, trying to sound casual.

He grinned. “We need more of those.”

That night’s session ran smoother. Deja read nearly a full chapter aloud. When she stumbled, Laneshia guided her gently through the words, letting her find her rhythm. Between the lessons, they talked about life. The struggle of paying bills, the small victories of motherhood, the absurdity of dating in Atlanta.

At one point, Deja said, “You don’t talk about yourself much.”

Laneshia smiled faintly. “Not much to tell.”

Deja raised an eyebrow. “That’s a lie.”

And Laneshia laughed. The sound softer than before.

From across the room, Malcolm watched them. He noticed the way Laneshia leaned in when Deja spoke. The way she listened with her whole body. He’d seen plenty of volunteers treat this work like charity. Like something to make themselves feel better. But not her. She gave attention like it was currency.

When class ended, he walked her to the parking lot. The night was cool. The air was heavy with the scent of rain and magnolia.

“You’ve got a gift,” he said as they reached her car.

She looked at him, confused. “A gift?”

“For making people believe they can do better.”

She opened her car door, uncertain how to respond. “I think that’s more Deja’s doing than mine.”

He shook his head. “Nah. You remind her it’s possible.”

Their eyes met again, that same quiet electricity between them. Not quite attraction. Not yet trust, but something that hummed with potential.

As she drove away, she thought of his words. Echoing faintly against the hum of her tires… *You remind her it’s possible.*

Maybe that was what she had come here for. To remind herself of the same thing.

By the third Thursday, Laneshia had stopped checking her watch during the sessions.
She no longer walked into the community center like a visitor but like someone who belonged there. Someone who understood the rhythm,

the chaos, the laughter, and the small triumphs stitched between the stumbles.

Deja was reading *The Bluest Eye* now, sounding out Morrison's words slowly and reverently like each syllable was a secret. Sometimes she'd pause and ask, "Ms. Laneshia, you ever feel like Pecola? Like you wanted to disappear so bad you forgot how to be seen?"

Laneshia never answered directly. She'd just smile, and say softly, "I think we all have those days."

But the truth was yes.
Yes, she'd felt that kind of invisibility.
Yes, she'd prayed to be unseen. To erase the parts of herself that hurt too much to carry.

The ache of memory lingered under her skin like an old scar. She'd grown up a church girl. Pressed and polished with a mother who believed silence was the holiest virtue and a father who believed appearance was salvation. By sixteen, Laneshia had learned that confession didn't always bring freedom. Sometimes it only brought shame.

She thought she'd left all that behind. But the smell of the coffee, the hum of community, even Malcolm's calm baritone reading of the Scripture before class… it all stirred something she'd buried.

That night, after the session ended, she lingered to help stack books. Rain pattered lightly against the windows. The kind that blurred the streetlights and made everything feel like a memory.

Malcolm was in the storage room, rearranging supplies. "You don't have to stay," he said when she stepped in. "I can finish up."

"I don't mind," she replied. "It's nice here after everyone's gone."

He smiled faintly. "You like quiet."

"Quiet's safe," she said before she could stop herself.

He looked at her. Then, really looked, and for a heartbeat, she felt seen in a way that was both comforting and terrifying.

"You ever notice," he said, "how sometimes quiet's just another kind of noise? The kind that keeps you from hearing what you don't want to?"

Her chest tightened. "You sound like a pastor."

He laughed softly. "Used to be. Long time ago."

Something in his tone made her turn. "What happened?"

He hesitated, leaning against the shelf. "Let's just say I stopped preaching when I realized I didn't always believe my own sermons."

Laneshia tilted her head. "And now?"

"Now I try to live 'em instead."

The words settled between them, heavy and honest.

She wanted to ask more. What broke his faith? How had he found his way back? She didn't. Some stories needed time to be invited out.

Instead, she said, "Well, you seem to be doing okay with that."

He smiled, a little sad. "Trying. Some days better than others."

Outside, thunder rolled faintly. He offered to walk her to her car, but she declined, pulling her umbrella from her bag. "I can handle a little rain," she said.

As she stepped into the drizzle, she felt his eyes on her. Not invasive, but protective, like he understood the small bravery it took just to keep showing up.

When she reached her car, she looked back. He was still standing in the doorway, arms crossed, watching until she drove off.

That night, she couldn't sleep. The sound of rain on her window carried her back to another storm…another time.

She was sixteen again. Sitting on the edge of her childhood bed in a cotton nightgown. The house thick with silence. Her mother's Bible lay open on the dresser, a verse underlined in red ink: **"Be still, and know that I am God."**

Back then, *stillness* had meant swallowing words. Hiding pain. Pretending holiness.

Now, as an adult, she realized how that silence had shaped her. It made her strong, yes, but brittle too. Always smiling. Always managing. Always hiding the tremor beneath the surface.

Her phone buzzed again. Another message from Malcolm.

"Heard it started pouring after you left. You make it home alright?"

She stared at it for a long moment before replying:

"Yes. Thank you. Just thinking too much."

"Thinking's good. Means something's waking up."

She typed back before she could second-guess herself:

"That's what scares me."

This time, the reply came slower.

"Good. The right kind of fear can mean healing's close."

She read that three times, her eyes stinging for reasons she couldn't name.

Then she whispered into the dark, barely audible, "I hope so."

The next Sunday, for the first time in years, Laneshia found herself walking into a church.

Not her old one. That was too haunted. This was a small storefront sanctuary near her apartment. its sign weathered and its pews mismatched.

The choir was off-key, the organ cracked, the preacher's mic fuzzy, but when the congregation sang *"Amazing Grace,"* something in her chest finally broke open.

Tears she didn't plan slid down her cheeks, and she didn't even wipe them away.

Because for the first time in a long time, it didn't feel like performance. It felt like return.

Chapter Two ~ What We Carry

Before Laneshia ever learned to doubt, she learned how to perform belief.

Sunday mornings in Southside Baptist started before sunrise. Her mother, Ruth Ann, would already be humming while she pressed Laneshia's white stockings against the ironing board, the hiss of steam rising like incense. The whole house smelled of starch, perfume, and Aqua Net. By the time they pulled into the church parking lot, the Georgia heat had already made the air shimmer.

The church sat at the end of a red-clay road, white clapboard siding, stained-glass windows, and a steeple that leaned just enough to make the deacons nervous every time the wind blew. Inside, ceiling fans stirred the air in slow, lazy circles. The ushers wore gloves, the choir swayed in their robes, and the tambourine kept time like a heartbeat.

Laneshia sat on the second pew from the front with her knees pressed together and her Bible balanced on her lap. She was fifteen and careful. Careful not to cross her legs, careful not to sing too loud, careful not to look bored.

"Keep your eyes on the pulpit, baby," her mother whispered whenever she caught Laneshia drifting. "The Lord sees everything."

That was how she understood God back then. Not as comfort, but as surveillance.

The church was her whole world.
It was where she learned how to be seen. Polished shoes, pleated skirts, "yes ma'am," "no sir." It was where she memorized Bible verses like spells and sang alto in the youth choir. Where she discovered that holiness came with a kind of applause if you learned the right rhythm.

The choir director, Sister Darlene, called her “our little saint.”
The pastor’s wife called her “an example.”
Her mother called her “my good girl.”

Laneshia wore those words like pearls. Pretty, fragile, and heavy around the neck.

But even then, she knew that goodness had a cost.

One Sunday afternoon, the heat was so thick that the church’s air-conditioning gave up halfway through service. Pastor Holt, back when he was still a booming young preacher with a gold ring that flashed when he waved his hand, kept preaching anyway. Sweat ran down his temples; the congregation fanned themselves with cardboard programs printed with funeral-home ads.

“Don’t you know,” he thundered, “that every trial you face is a test of your faith?”

Laneshia’s father, Raymond, shouted “Amen!” so loud the pew rattled. He was a deacon then, proud of his voice, proud of his family. The picture of righteousness in a pinstripe suit.

After the benediction, the grown-ups lingered in the fellowship hall, gossiping over sweet tea and deviled eggs. The kids ran outside to play tag in the church yard, their laughter cutting through the drone of cicadas.

Laneshia sat under the oak tree, her white socks already collecting red dust. She opened her Bible, pretending to read. She didn’t want to play. She liked watching the movement, the noise, the way sunlight slipped between branches.

“Always studying, huh?”

The voice made her jump. It was Tyrone, one of the older boys from youth choir. Seventeen, smooth-talking, and always smiling with too much confidence.

She smiled shyly. “Trying to stay out of trouble.”

He laughed. “Trouble got a way of finding you anyway.”

Something in his tone made her uncomfortable, though she couldn’t have said why. He sat down beside her, close enough for her to feel his cologne — sharp and sweet.

Before she could think of what to say, her mother called from the fellowship hall, “Laneshia! Come help with these dishes!”

She jumped up quickly, murmuring a polite “bye,” and ran inside.

That night, as she lay in bed, she replayed the moment in her mind. The way his eyes had lingered, the way her pulse had quickened with something she didn’t understand.

She told herself it was nothing. That she was overreacting.
That good girls didn’t feel fear without reason.

A week later, the church bus took the youth choir to a revival in Macon. The girls sat in the back, singing along to the radio, while the adults gossiped up front. Laneshia stared out the window, tracing raindrops as they raced down the glass.

Beside her, her best friend, Janelle, whispered, “You think Pastor Holt ever gets tired of talking?”

Laneshia giggled. “Probably not. He likes the sound of his own voice too much.”

They stifled their laughter as the bus rolled on, thunder rumbling in the distance.

When they arrived, the sky broke open, rain hammering the church roof. Inside, the congregation shouted and sang, tambourines clapping like lightning. Laneshia sang too, voice trembling with joy she couldn’t quite name. She loved those moments. The unity…the surrender. For a little while, she believed every word.

But later that night, when the service ended and the adults lingered in prayer circles, she slipped outside for air. The rain had stopped, and the night smelled of wet earth and honeysuckle.

She heard footsteps behind her. Tyrone again.

"You sounded good tonight," he said.

"Thanks," she replied, wrapping her arms around herself.

He smiled, stepping closer. "You too holy to talk to me?"

She shook her head. "Just tired."

He studied her for a long moment, then said quietly, "Don't let them make you think you gotta be perfect all the time."

Something in her stomach twisted. Confusion…curiosity…fear.

Before she could respond, Sister Ruth's voice rang out from inside, calling her name. Laneshia exhaled in relief and hurried toward the door.

That night, she couldn't sleep. Something had shifted. Not because of what happened, but because of what *almost* did.

It was the first time she realized how thin the line was between safety and danger, between faith and denial. Years later, she'd remember that summer as the beginning of her silence. Not the silence that came from obedience, but the silence that came from learning how easily people looked away.

Ruth Ann was a church woman. Pious, devout, and terrifying in equal measure. She believed in discipline, in obedience, and in the power of words to shape souls. Laneshia learned early that mistakes were not forgiven lightly and that disappointment could twist a mother's face into a mask of sharp angles and cold silence. Ruth Ann often reminded her daughter that life was a test and that only the pure of heart would be spared suffering. But Laneshia wondered if purity mattered when it seemed so selective. Favoring her older brother, Terrence, every single time.

Terrence had his father's easy charm and her mother's cunning smile. He could do no wrong in the eyes of anyone who mattered. Churchgoers, neighbors, even teachers. And in his shadow, Laneshia learned to shrink. She learned to laugh when he laughed, to nod when he spoke, to pretend her feelings were invisible.

But there were moments in the dark that no one else saw.

When her brother's footsteps crept down the hall at night, when the latch on her bedroom door rattled softly, Laneshia felt something shift inside her chest. A mixture of fear, confusion, and helplessness that she did not yet have the words to name. She began to pray quietly in the dark, murmuring fragments of scripture she barely understood, hoping that God, if He was listening, would intervene. She squeezed her eyes shut until they ached, counting the seconds until morning.

Her mother never knew.

And if she had, Laneshia suspected Ruth Ann would have dismissed her with a sharp word or a hand slapped across the back of her head.

One summer afternoon, while the sun poured its heat over the yard like molten gold, Laneshia tried to speak. She stammered, tried to explain the fear that followed her, the way she could not breathe freely in her own home. But Ruth Ann's voice cut her off like a blade.

"You watch your filthy mouth," she snapped, eyes flashing. "That boy is a man of God. Don't you ever speak lies like that again."

After that, Laneshia stopped trying. She became quiet. Too quiet. Folding herself into the corners of her life where no one would notice. She spoke only when spoken to. Smiled only when required. And learned that survival sometimes meant pretending that everything was normal.

Yet, even in the midst of darkness, there were small lights. Her grandmother's stories about the old family in Georgia. The smell of fresh biscuits on Sunday mornings. The fleeting laughter she shared with neighborhood friends. These were her refuge. They reminded her that the world was larger than the house that confined her, that life could be more than survival.

By the time Laneshia turned eighteen, the Stanson house had become a cage she could no longer tolerate. She packed a small duffel bag with a few dresses, her high school diploma, the Bible she wasn't sure she still believed in, and caught a bus north to Atlanta. She did not look back. The city, with its roar of traffic, neon lights, and endless possibilities, promised a kind of freedom she had never known.

As the bus rumbled down the highway, Laneshia pressed her forehead against the window. Watching the Georgia trees blur into the distance. She felt a strange mix of fear and exhilaration. She was leaving behind everything familiar and maybe, she thought, that was exactly what she needed to find herself.

But freedom, she would soon discover, had its own chains.

She didn't have words for it yet.
But she carried it anyway.

By the time the air cooled enough for evening service, the cicadas had surrendered their chorus to crickets. The white clapboard church stood beneath a bruised-purple sky, its steeple cutting against the sunset like a small promise. Inside, the smell of powder, starch, and perfume mixed with sweat and the faint tang of Pine-Sol.

Laneshia smoothed the hem of her Sunday dress, peach-colored with a white collar and followed her mother down the aisle. Ruth Ann's heels struck the floorboards in measured rhythm, the sound of order and command. People turned to greet them with polite smiles, but Laneshia could feel the weight of their eyes shift subtly: from her mother's immaculate hat to Laneshia's nervous hands.

The church was both comfort and cage. Here, she knew every song, every scripture, every gesture. Here, she could anticipate the swell of the organ before the choir rose. But she also knew the rules too well. How to keep her voice soft, her knees together, her questions tucked neatly behind her teeth.

Tonight, Pastor Wiggins preached about obedience. About how a daughter's duty was to reflect her mother's virtue. His words slid across the congregation like oil, heavy and hard to wash off. Ruth Ann nodded fiercely, as though the sermon had been written for her alone. Laneshia sat still, her fingers tracing the grooves in the wooden pew, feeling the pressure of expectation like a hand on her shoulder.

After service, the fellowship hall smelled of pound cake and lemonade. Church ladies in floral dresses clustered around Ruth Ann, complimenting her hat and praising Terrence for helping with the collection plates. Laneshia lingered near the edge of the crowd, half-seen, her smile small and dutiful.

"Chile, you quiet as a mouse," Sister Geneva teased, pinching her cheek. "You gone be a good wife one day. Ain't no man like a woman that don't talk too much."

Everyone laughed. Even her mother.

Laneshia forced a smile. She had learned early that laughter could protect her; it disguised discomfort better than silence.

Later, when the fellowship ended and the church lights dimmed, she slipped outside before her mother noticed. The night air clung to her skin, humid and heavy. The gravel crunched beneath her shoes as she walked toward the small clearing beside the churchyard where the grass grew high and the stars felt closer.

She sat on the low stone wall, clutching her small purse to her lap. From inside the church, she could still hear the muffled echoes of choir chatter and laughter. It was strange, how the same songs that once made her feel close to God now sounded like something distant, unreachable.

She closed her eyes and whispered a question she would never have dared to ask aloud:
"Why do I feel so small in Your house?"

The wind rustled through the trees, carrying no answer. Only the hum of the earth and the steady beating of her own heart.

Behind her, the church doors creaked open. She turned to see Deacon Hayes step into the darkness, his white shirt glowing faintly under the porch light. He was one of the church elders—older, respected, the kind of man her mother trusted without question.

"Evenin', baby girl," he said, his voice warm, practiced. "You out here all by yourself?"

Laneshia straightened, unsure why her stomach tightened. "Just getting some air."

He chuckled softly, stepping closer. "Ain't nothin' wrong with that. But you be careful now. Lotta danger in the dark."

His tone carried something she couldn't name, and though his words were kind, they left a chill in the air. When her mother called from inside, Laneshia nearly sighed in relief.

That night, lying in bed, she stared at the ceiling fan as it turned lazily overhead. Her mother's voice drifted through the thin wall, laughing with Terrence. The sound made her chest ache.

In that moment, she began to understand something she wouldn't have words for until years later. Danger didn't always come as thunder. Sometimes it came as silence. As trust misplaced. As a child, learning that being quiet was safer than being believed.

She closed her eyes and whispered the same question again, softer this time:
"Why do I feel so small in Your house?"

There was no answer. Only the hum of the fan, the weight of Sunday, and the quiet beginning of doubt.

Ruth Ann Stanson believed in order.

The kind that kept the world from crumbling, that held a woman upright when everything inside her wanted to collapse. She believed in pressed clothes, clean floors, and children who said “yes ma’am” without rolling their eyes. To her, obedience was next to holiness. Maybe even above it. Because holiness, she’d learned, could come and go but order could keep a family from shame.

On Sunday nights, when the last hymn faded and the church lights went dark, Ruth Ann would come home and stand by the kitchen window. The sink was always spotless, the counters cleared. She’d pour herself a small glass of sweet tea and watch the moon rise over the pine trees. That was the only time she let herself think.

Sometimes she remembered her own mama. Sharp-tongued, God-fearing, and unyielding. A woman who could quote scripture as easily as she could deliver punishment. Back then, Ruth Ann hadn’t understood how fear could live inside love. But now, raising two children on a teacher’s salary and the grace of God, she understood all too well.

She carried a quiet terror that the world would swallow them whole.

Terrence was easy. Bright, charming, a natural in the eyes of everyone who mattered. He had his father’s smile, the same one that had first convinced Ruth Ann to overlook the warnings. But Laneshia… her daughter was different. Too soft, too thoughtful. The kind of girl who felt everything too deeply. And deep feeling, Ruth Ann knew, was dangerous.

“Feeling don’t feed you,” she told her daughter once. “Discipline does.”

Still, sometimes, like tonight, she caught a glimpse of Laneshia’s face in the church light, and something in her chest tightened. The child’s eyes had begun to hold that distant, searching look Ruth Ann remembered from her own reflection long ago.

She told herself it was just adolescence. Growing pains.

But late at night, when the house was quiet, Ruth Ann would wake from half-dreams filled with voices. Her mother's, her pastor's, her own. Each one reminding her that good mothers raised obedient children. Good mothers didn't let the world see cracks.

If something was wrong, you prayed it away. You fixed it before anyone found out.

She never asked Laneshia the hard questions. Never looked too closely when the girl flinched or grew quiet after church events. She didn't know how to face the possibility that faith might not be protection after all.

So she prayed harder. Cleaned more. Tightened the rules.

Maybe, she thought, if she built the walls high enough, God would not notice the fear living inside her house.

From her bedroom, Laneshia sometimes heard her mother pacing at night. The slow rhythm of footsteps across the floorboards sounded like a metronome—steady, anxious, endless. She didn't know what her mother prayed for, but she could feel the tension in the air, like a string pulled too tight.

In the mornings, Ruth Ann acted as though nothing had happened. She'd fry bacon, hum hymns, and fuss about the dishes. But Laneshia saw the exhaustion behind her mother's eyes. The way her hands trembled slightly when she reached for her coffee cup

It was strange, Laneshia thought, how silence could be inherited.

She began writing little prayers on scraps of notebook paper, folding them neatly, and slipping them under her pillow. Most were just a few words: *Help me understand. Keep Mama from hurting. Let me be good.*

She wasn't sure who would read them. God, angels, or nobody at all—but the act of writing felt like a secret form of survival.

By late summer, the first whispers of adulthood began to find her. The kind that comes not through milestones, but through awareness. The realization that protection was never guaranteed.

She stopped asking certain questions at church. Stopped expecting answers from the people who smiled the hardest. And for the first time, she began to imagine a life beyond the Stanson house, beyond the small town that held her history like a secret.

In her journal, she wrote:
One day I'll leave, and maybe then, I'll finally breathe.

Chapter Three ~ The Leaving Kind

The summer she turned eighteen, the heat came early and stayed late. By June, the air in Willow Ridge felt thick enough to drink. Sunlight poured itself over the cracked pavement, the cicadas screamed from dawn till night, and every porch fan spun like it was trying to outrun time.

Laneshia had graduated two weeks before. The ceremony had been held in the high school gym. The kind of place where the walls still smelled faintly of chalk and sweat. Ruth Ann cried quietly during the principal's speech, dabbing her eyes with a handkerchief, and afterward told anyone who'd listen, "My baby headed to Atlanta. Gonna make something of herself."

Laneshia smiled and let her mother have that moment. But inside, she felt more uncertain than proud. Leaving home was something she had prayed for since she was thirteen. Now that it was real, the freedom scared her.

She had been accepted to Spelman College on a partial scholarship, a miracle she still didn't quite believe. The acceptance letter sat folded inside her Bible, tucked between Psalms and Proverbs like a secret blessing. She'd read it so many times that the paper had grown soft at the creases.

Atlanta.

Even the word felt like possibility. A place big enough to hold her questions, her dreams, and the pieces of herself that never quite fit in Willow Ridge.

But the leaving wasn't clean.

Her mother spent the weeks before departure moving through the house like a woman preparing for battle. Every drawer reorganized, every bed sheet washed twice, every conversation threaded with unspoken fear.

“You stay prayed up, you hear?” Ruth Ann said one night, ironing Laneshia’s blouses. “That city’ll chew you up if you forget who you are.”

Laneshia nodded. “Yes ma’am.”

“You don’t trust nobody you just meet. Not boys, not girls, not even them church folks. They smile at you one minute and talk about you the next.”

“Yes ma’am.”

“And if you ever need to come home, you come home. Don’t let pride keep you out there struggling.”

Laneshia didn’t answer that one. She couldn’t promise what she didn’t believe.

That night, after her mother went to bed, she stood at her window and looked out over the quiet neighborhood. The same porch lights, the same barking dog, the same stars. She had always wondered what it would feel like to leave them behind. And now, standing in the dim light, she realized she wasn’t escaping so much as transforming.

She whispered the same words she had written years before:
Help me understand.
Only now, the prayer sounded less like a plea and more like a vow.

A week later, Terrence drove her to the Greyhound station in his old Buick. The car smelled like motor oil and peppermint gum. He had grown into himself since high school. Taller, broader, his voice deep with a quiet authority that still caught her off guard.

“You sure you ready for this?” he asked as they idled at a red light.

Laneshia smiled faintly. “If I wait till I’m ready, I’ll never go.”

He nodded, drumming his fingers on the steering wheel. “Mama gon’ have a fit once you gone.”

“I know.”

“You call me if she act up too much, you hear? I’ll check on her.”

Laneshia looked out the window, her throat tightening.

When they reached the station, he carried her suitcase to the bus door and stood there awkwardly, shifting his weight from one foot to the other.

“Don’t forget where you from,” he said finally. “But don’t let where you from tell you who you are.”

She wanted to hug him, but instead she just nodded. The bus hissed, the door folded open, and the driver called out for passengers bound for Atlanta.

Laneshia climbed aboard, found a window seat, and pressed her forehead against the glass.

As the bus pulled away, she watched the town shrink into distance. The church steeple, the water tower, the rows of cotton fields blurring into green and gold. Her reflection shimmered faintly in the window. A girl becoming a woman, a believer becoming something else.

She didn’t know what was waiting for her in the city. But for the first time, she didn’t feel small.

She felt ready.

Atlanta smelled like rain and ambition.

The Greyhound hissed to a stop under the faded awning of the downtown terminal, and when Laneshia stepped off, the air hit her like a different kind of heat. Wet, electric, and humming with possibility. Buses growled in every direction, people hurried past with headphones and coffee cups, and the city seemed to move on its own rhythm. A heartbeat faster than anything she'd known.

She clutched her single suitcase and followed the crowd toward the street. The sky was bruised with clouds, but even the threat of rain couldn't dim the shine of the skyline. Steel and glass rose around her like a promise. "*You're not home anymore",* she thought.

Her cousin Joy met her at the curb in a silver Toyota with the windows rolled down and music pulsing from the speakers, SWV, loud enough to make heads turn.

"Look at you!" Joy shouted, grinning. "Little country girl all grown up!"

Laneshia laughed despite herself and climbed in. Joy was everything she wasn't. Bold, confident, hair dyed honey-blonde and styled high. She'd been living in Atlanta since finishing community college and had offered to host Laneshia for the summer before classes began.

"You gon' love it here," Joy said, merging into traffic. "Ain't nothin' like Atlanta in the summer. Everybody out, everybody lookin' good, everybody tryna make somethin' happen."

Laneshia stared out the window as the city flashed past billboards, food trucks, people in bright clothes walking with purpose. Even the air smelled alive! Fried catfish, car exhaust, and blooming magnolia!

At Joy's apartment, a narrow brick building near Cascade Road, Laneshia unpacked. Slowly folding her few clothes into a dresser that stuck on the second drawer. From the window she could see downtown glittering in the distance. Lights flickering like restless prayers.

That night, the city's hum followed her into sleep.

The next morning, Joy took her on a tour of the neighborhood.

They passed barbershops blasting gospel and hip-hop in equal measure, corner stores where men stood laughing near the ice chest, beauty salons perfumed with burnt hair and ambition. Everywhere, people were moving! Working, hustling, shining.

"You see that right there?" Joy said, pointing to a storefront where a woman sold custom wigs. "She started out in her mama's kitchen. Now she owns two locations. You can make somethin' happen here if you ain't scared to move."

Laneshia nodded, feeling the pulse of the city in her chest.

But that night, when Joy went out with friends, Laneshia stayed home. She sat at the small kitchen table, journal open, listening to the faint music drifting from passing cars. The quiet felt different here. Lonely, but alive.

She wrote:
The city don't wait for you to figure it out. It just keeps moving, and you decide whether to move with it or get left behind.

Classes started two weeks later.

At Spelman, everything gleamed. The red brick buildings, the manicured lawns, the confident young women who spoke with purpose. Laneshia felt both inspired and invisible. Professors quoted Morrison and Baldwin like scripture; students debated theology and justice as easily as breathing.

She loved it and feared it.

In chapel one morning, a guest speaker said, "Faith isn't about silence. It's about speaking truth in the face of power."

Laneshia wrote that down. Later, in her dorm, she read it over and over. It felt like someone had opened a window she hadn't known was there.

By mid-semester, she began to shed her old skin. She cut her hair shorter, started wearing jeans instead of dresses, and found herself sitting in the back of the campus church. Not out of rebellion, but out of a need to see things from a different angle.

When she called home on Sundays, Ruth Ann's voice carried both pride and distance.

"You keep goin' to service, right?"

"Yes ma'am."

"And you pray before bed?"

"Every night."

But sometimes Laneshia hung up the phone and sat staring at the cross above her desk, wondering if prayer meant the same thing here as it did back home.

In Atlanta, faith didn't seem to mean quiet. It meant questioning. And maybe, she thought, that was its own kind of holiness.

By sophomore year, the city had claimed her rhythm.

She walked faster now, spoke louder, laughed easier. She'd learned which bus line to take to campus, which corner store sold the best peach soda, and which streets to avoid after dark. She'd learned that Atlanta could love you and test you in the same breath.

Her roommate, Kendra, was a sociology major from Chicago. Sharp, funny, and fearless. She wore hoop earrings the size of teacups and kept a Bible on her nightstand next to a stack of Zora Neale Hurston books.

"You still goin' to church every Sunday?" Kendra asked one morning as they got dressed.

"Most Sundays," Laneshia said, pulling her hair into a bun.

Kendra grinned. "You sound like you negotiatin' with God."

"Maybe I am."

They both laughed, but the truth was, church no longer felt like it used to. The hymns were familiar, but her heart was different. She no longer sought forgiveness so much as understanding.

In her religion class, she read theologians who spoke about faith as protest, as healing, as art. One evening, while writing a paper, she found herself scribbling in the margins of her notes:

Maybe salvation ain't about being spotless. Maybe it's about being seen.

She didn't show that line to anyone, but it stayed with her.

During spring semester, Laneshia joined a campus poetry collective called **The Listening Room.** It met every Thursday night in the basement of the student center. The air was thick with incense and words.

The first time she read one of her poems aloud, her voice trembled. The piece was called *Sunday Dress*. A meditation on silence and survival. When she finished, the room stayed quiet for a long moment before someone snapped their fingers in rhythm.

Kendra grinned from the front row. “Told you, girl. You got fire in that voice.”

That night, walking back to the dorm, Laneshia felt lighter. For the first time, she understood that storytelling could be a form of prayer too. A way to speak what she had been trained to hide.

By her final year, she had learned to move between worlds. The faithful and the free. The holy and the human.

She interned at a nonprofit downtown tutoring girls from neighborhoods that reminded her of home. She told them, “You don’t have to be perfect to be worthy.” Some of them rolled their eyes, but a few nodded, the way she used to when someone said something she wasn’t ready to believe yet.

She stopped straightening her hair. Started volunteering at open-mic nights. Began keeping a small notebook of prayers rewritten as poems.

When Ruth Ann came to visit for graduation, she stood in Laneshia’s apartment doorway, eyes wide at the posters on the wall. Toni Morrison, Audre Lorde, and a print that read *Faith is not the absence of doubt.*

Ruth Ann frowned slightly. “You still believe, don’t you?”

Laneshia smiled softly. “More than ever, Mama. Just... different now.”

Her mother didn’t answer right away. She touched one of the framed poems and whispered, “You always did have a strange way of talkin’ to God.”

That night, after her mother went to bed, Laneshia sat on the balcony overlooking the city lights. She thought of the little girl who once whispered into the dark, *Why do I feel so small in Your house?*

Now she felt the same question, but it no longer hurt. It simply *was.* A part of her faith, not a failure of it.

She opened her notebook and wrote one final line before bed:
I am still that church girl, but I’m learning that lost and found can live in the same body.

Chapter Four ~ Eden in the City

The year 2002 began with the smell of rain on red clay and the sound of church bells echoing faintly from somewhere downtown.

Laneshia stood at her apartment window, watching the city wake up. From five stories above Peachtree Street, the world looked soft. Cars like toy models, people walking fast with coffee cups and sunlight stretching across glass buildings.

She was twenty-two and, for the first time in her life, completely on her own.

Her apartment was small. One room, one window, and one stubborn radiator that clanked like it had complaints of its own. But it was hers. No one told her to turn down her music or press her clothes or be home before dark. Freedom, she realized, had its own quiet soundtrack. Humming refrigerators, distant sirens…the rustle of her own breath.

She had a job at a nonprofit arts center called *The Wellhouse*, a small space wedged between a church and a soul food café. They ran afterschool programs for girls with writing workshops, art classes, and open mics on Friday nights.

It wasn't glamorous, but it felt like purpose.

Every morning, she arrived early, sweeping the floors before the students came, unlocking the supply closet that smelled of markers and dust. On the walls hung collages of bright paper and quotes from poets: *"The truth will set you free, but first it will piss you off." – Gloria Steinem.*

Sometimes she caught herself whispering that one under her breath.

In the evenings, after the last student left, she'd stay behind to write. Her notebook had become a second home, a place where her faith and frustration met halfway.

She wrote about the city's rhythm. The gospel radio stations that faded into R&B. The preachers who sounded like poets and the poets who sounded like preachers. She wrote about the women she saw on the bus. Tired, beautiful, and carrying whole worlds in their purses.

And sometimes she wrote about herself, though not by name. She called her stand-in "L," a woman always walking toward something she couldn't quite name.

Sundays were still for church, though now she chose which one. She had tried a few megachurches with lights and cameras, small ones tucked into storefronts, but she hadn't yet found the place that felt right.

One rainy morning, she ducked into a service near Auburn Avenue just to get out of the weather. The sign outside read *New Hope Fellowship.* Inside, the air was thick with incense and the choir sang a slow, haunting version of "His Eye Is on the Sparrow."

Something about it hit her square in the chest.

The pastor, a woman with silver locs and eyes that saw straight through you, spoke that day about wandering.

"Sometimes the lost ones are the closest to grace," she said. "Because they still looking."

Laneshia sat still, rainwater drying on her sleeves, feeling as if the words had been waiting for her.

That afternoon, she walked home under a clearing sky, the city shining like it had just been baptized. She passed a mural she hadn't noticed before. Bright pink roses breaking through concrete, their petals stretching toward painted sunlight. Beneath them, someone had scrawled in looping letters:

LAADIE OHH.

She smiled without knowing why. Maybe it was the name, or the defiance of beauty blooming where it wasn't supposed to. She stopped, traced a finger over the rough paint, and whispered, "Still growing."

It felt like a prayer.

The first time Laneshia saw **Jamal Pierce**, he was painting a wall.

It was a Saturday afternoon at *The Wellhouse*, one of those volunteer workdays when the staff and community showed up to freshen the space. Music pulsed low from a Bluetooth speaker. Old-school soul, warm and steady. Jamal stood on a ladder, paintbrush in hand, streaking the upper corner of the wall with broad, confident strokes. His T-shirt was flecked with white paint, his jeans faded and loose around the knees.

He looked down and grinned. "You mind passing that roller, miss artist?"

"I'm not an artist," she said automatically, handing it over.

"Anybody who shows up to help create something new is an artist," he replied. "You just don't know your medium yet."

She laughed. A little caught off guard by his easy charm.

Jamal wasn't conventionally handsome. His nose slightly crooked, a small scar above his eyebrow, but his smile was full of light. The kind that made you believe people could be good again. He had grown up in Decatur, studied design at a community college, and now ran a small mural collective that worked with teens around the city.

Over the next few weeks, they kept crossing paths. Sometimes he dropped by *The Wellhouse* to check on his students. Other times he brought her coffee when she stayed late to write grants or plan workshops.

One evening, he found her sitting at her desk long after closing, staring at a blank page in frustration.

"Writer's block?" he asked, leaning against the doorway.

"Life block," she muttered.

He chuckled. "You know, sometimes you gotta stop trying to make sense of things and just paint over 'em. Start fresh."

“I don’t paint,” she said again.

“You should,” he answered simply. “It’s like praying without words.”

That line stayed with her.

A week later, she joined one of his Saturday youth workshops. He handed her a brush, a jar of blue paint, and told her to fill a section of the wall with “whatever she was feeling.”

She hesitated, then dipped the brush and dragged a trembling streak across the plaster. It felt… liberating. Like exhaling something she hadn’t realized she’d been holding.

By the end of the afternoon, the wall bloomed with color! Swirls of red, gold, turquoise, and lavender. Her section was messy, unsure, but alive.

“You see?” Jamal said, nodding. “That’s what healing looks like before it makes sense.”

They began seeing more of each other outside of work. Dinners at small restaurants. Walks through Little Five Points. Hours sitting by the Chattahoochee River, watching the water move like time itself. Slow, relentless, and cleansing.

He listened when she spoke. Not the way Malcolm once had, with charisma and quiet calculation, but with real presence.

Sometimes she caught herself pulling back, waiting for the other shoe to drop, for the hidden sermon or subtle manipulation. But Jamal didn’t preach. He didn’t quote scripture to sound wise. When he talked about faith, it came wrapped in humility.

“God don’t need us to be perfect,” he said one night, tossing a stone into the river. “Just real.”

At *The Wellhouse*, Laneshia's confidence grew. The girls in her writing program began to blossom under her care. They wrote poems about fathers who disappeared, mothers who worked too much, and dreams of becoming something no one expected.

One afternoon, a shy girl named Amara handed her a folded sheet of paper.

"I wrote this after class," she whispered.

Laneshia opened it later, alone. The poem began:

Miss L say we ain't broken / just under renovation
and I believe her / 'cause she say it like she know.

Laneshia pressed the paper to her chest and cried. Quietly. Not from sadness, but from recognition.

She *did* know.

Still, not everything was soft and healing. Atlanta had its edges. Money was tight, and her landlord had begun raising rent. The nonprofit struggled with funding, and her boss, a tired woman named Ms. Carter, warned her that layoffs were coming.

And then, one rainy Thursday, a letter arrived from her mother.

Ruth Ann's handwriting was sharp, tight, almost angry on the page.

Heard you living in sin up there in that city. Heard you left church. God sees everything, Laneshia. Come home before He reminds you who you are.

Laneshia read it twice, folded it neatly, and placed it in a drawer. For the first time, the guilt didn't stick. The words rolled off her like water from paint that had already dried.

She whispered to the silence, “I already know who I am, Mama.”

That night, she sat at her window again. The city shimmered below. Headlights moving like fireflies and rain slicking the streets.

She picked up her notebook and began to write.

There are no angels here. Just women learning how to breathe again.

And for the first time in years, she felt something close to peace. Not the loud, performative kind preached from pulpits, but the quiet, personal kind you find in your own reflection.

Spring rolled into the kind of summer that felt endless. Thick air, slow days, and the hum of Atlanta wrapped in heat. *The Wellhouse* was buzzing with energy. New teens, new grants, new possibilities. But beneath the surface, cracks had begun to show.

Budgets were tightening again. Ms. Carter started skipping meetings, her face drawn with worry. The landlord of their building had raised the lease, and whispers of "closure" traveled like smoke.

Laneshia stayed late most nights, writing proposal after proposal, praying, though she no longer used that word, for a miracle. The work mattered to her. These kids…this space. It wasn't just a job. It was redemption.

She told Jamal one evening as they sat on the hood of his car outside her apartment.

"If they close The Wellhouse," she said, "it'll feel like losing a piece of me."

He nodded, silent for a while. Then, softly, "Sometimes the things we build aren't meant to last forever. They just teach us how to build better next time."

She wanted to believe him, but part of her still carried that Southern ache—the one that made her think faith was something you *held onto*, not something you *grew through*.

A few weeks later, the board made it official: *The Wellhouse* would shut its doors by the end of the year.

The staff gathered in the meeting room, the air heavy with disappointment. Ms. Carter tried to sound hopeful. "We'll help the kids transition to other programs," she said. But everyone knew what that meant. Another dream, another promise…quietly dying.

That night, Laneshia walked home in silence. The city lights blurred through her tears, and she thought of all the voices that had filled that building. The laughter, the stories, the courage.

She wrote in her journal:

We plant seeds even when we know we won't see the garden.

Jamal showed up later that evening with takeout and two bottles of ginger ale.

"No sermons tonight," he said, setting the food down. "Just food and quiet."

They ate in near silence, the soft hum of Miles Davis floating in the background.

"Maybe it's time to do something different," Jamal said finally. "Start your own program. Write. Speak. People listen to you."

She shook her head. "I wouldn't even know where to begin."

He smiled. "You already did. Every time you told one of those girls they mattered, you were building something."

She didn't answer, but his words sank deep.

As summer faded, their relationship deepened in small, meaningful ways. They learned each other's silences. Theirs wasn't a love of fireworks, but of quiet endurance.

Still, sometimes when he reached for her hand, she hesitated.

It wasn't him she didn't trust. It was the feeling of being seen too clearly.

One night, as they walked along the BeltLine, he stopped suddenly.

"You ever think about what you want, Laneshia? Not what you're supposed to want. What *you* want?"

The question caught her off guard.

"I want peace," she said finally. "And maybe… to matter."

He smiled gently. "You already do. You just don't believe it yet."

Then came the call.

Ms. Carter had suffered a mild stroke. The board asked Laneshia to temporarily manage The Wellhouse until it officially closed.

She accepted without hesitation, though the weight of it pressed on her. She handled the logistics. Closing accounts, archiving files, and helping teens find new programs. But it broke her heart to pack away the poetry journals, the artwork, the dreams.

On the final day, she walked through the empty space one last time. The walls, once alive with color and laughter, stood bare. Only faint streaks of paint remained. Reminders of the lives that had passed through.

She found her section of the mural, the one she'd painted years ago with Jamal. The blue streak still shimmered faintly in the light.

She touched it and whispered, "Thank you."

Not to the building. Not to the city. But to the version of herself who had dared to try again.

That night, Jamal came by.

"I saw the lights off when I drove past," he said. "You okay?"

She nodded, tears glimmering in her eyes. "Yeah. I think so. I'm just… tired."

He took her hand. “Then rest. But don’t stop. There’s more in you, L.”

She looked at him, realizing how far she’d come. From silence and shame to this quiet, steady hope.

“Maybe,” she said softly, “but I’m not sure what comes next.”

“Then let’s find out together.”

And for the first time, she didn’t flinch when someone said *together.*

Chapter Five ~The Gospel of Work

Atlanta, 2008.

The city pulsed with change. New cranes on the skyline, fresh condos rising where old brick warehouses once stood. Everyone was chasing something. Money, relevance, escape. And somewhere in that hum of motion was Laneshia, thirty years old, learning how to worship in a new kind of church.

The altar was a desk.
The hymns were Slack pings and email threads.
The prayers were silent, typed in code and deadlines.

After *The Wellhouse* closed, she'd drifted for a while—freelancing, tutoring, writing when she could. But the bills didn't stop coming, and Atlanta was no place for sentimentality. Eventually, she landed an entry-level communications job at a growing tech firm called **DynaCore Systems**.

At first, she felt like an imposter. Everyone around her seemed fluent in a language she barely understood—scrums, UX flows, scalability, product roadmaps. But she learned fast. Laneshia had always been fluent in adaptation.

She took online courses at night, watched tutorials until her eyes blurred, and within two years had become one of DynaCore's most reliable project managers.

Work became her rhythm.
Precision her prayer.
Control her comfort.

Her office was sleek and sterile. All glass and steel. A world away from the chipped paint and loud laughter of *The Wellhouse*.

But there was something about the order of it that soothed her. No chaos. No emotion spilling out of the walls. Just metrics, milestones, and measurable success.

She told herself it was growth. Maturity. Maybe even healing.

Still, there were moments when she caught herself staring out the window of the twenty-third floor, wondering when survival had become her only language.

At church, when she occasionally went, people liked to say "God gives you new seasons." But Laneshia had begun to think seasons weren't gifts. They were exchanges. You gave up something to enter a new one.

At *The Wellhouse*, she'd given her heart.
At DynaCore, she'd given her peace.

She didn't realize how deep the trade had gone until her body started warning her. Sleepless nights. Tightness in her chest. A kind of quiet exhaustion that coffee couldn't fix.

She'd once believed burnout was for people who didn't pray enough. Now she knew it was just what happened when you kept saying *yes* to everything except yourself.

Her new manager, **Ava Morales**, was sharp and precise, the kind of woman who made competence look like art. Ava saw something in Laneshia early on. Maybe it was her discipline or maybe her empathy, either way, she began pulling her into high-stakes projects.

"Don't shrink to make people comfortable," Ava told her one afternoon after a tough client call. "If you know your worth, speak like it."

Laneshia took that to heart.

Soon she was leading presentations, negotiating contracts, and managing cross-functional teams. She dressed the part too! Tailored blazers, pointed heels, and a controlled grace that looked effortless even when it wasn't.

People at work called her "steady." They didn't see the nights she came home and sat in the dark, scrolling through old photos of murals, poetry workshops, and children's laughter.

She told herself that life was gone. That version of her had been too soft, too idealistic.

But sometimes, just before sleep, she still dreamed in color. Paint on her hands, Jamal's laughter echoing down a hallway that no longer existed.

One Friday, as she left the office late, she saw a familiar face outside a coffee shop.

Jamal.

He looked older, calmer, still carrying that quiet light. His hair had a few gray strands now, his smile just as easy.

"L?" he said, eyes widening in surprise.

She laughed softly. "Didn't expect to see you here."

"I could say the same. Thought you were allergic to this side of town," he teased.

They sat down over coffee, catching up. He was still running community art programs, expanding them into local schools. She told him about her work. Strategic launches, brand campaigns, late nights.

"You sound… successful," he said, with a mix of pride and concern.

"I am," she replied. Then, quieter: "I think."

He looked at her for a long moment. “You ever miss it? The work you used to do?”

She stared out the window. The city reflected in the glass. “Sometimes. But missing doesn’t pay rent.”

He nodded, not arguing. Just understanding.

When they said goodbye, he hugged her gently, the kind of embrace that didn’t ask for anything. But as she walked away, something inside her stirred. An ache she’d buried under spreadsheets and structure.

That night, she opened her old notebook for the first time in years. The pages smelled faintly of dust and memory.

She wrote just one line:

I built a new life out of logic and light, but my heart still speaks in paint.

Then she closed it, not ready to face the rest.

By 2011, Laneshia had become a name people mentioned in meetings. Not whispered…not doubted…..*mentioned*.

“Let Laneshia lead it.”
“Loop Laneshia in. She’ll fix it.”

It was the recognition she’d once prayed for without knowing what it would cost.

Her corner of DynaCore’s office was sleek. Floor-to-ceiling windows, a plant she kept alive mostly by accident, and a corkboard filled with color-coded timelines. She was good at this life. Too good.

Ava promoted her to Senior Program Manager that spring. Along with the title came more money, more power, and more silence. Because when you climb high enough, there are fewer people to talk to.

The project that changed everything came a few months later: **Atlas**, an internal data platform designed to optimize user behavior for DynaCore’s clients. It was brilliant, lucrative and ethically murky.

Laneshia noticed it first in a spreadsheet. Data points tagged to personal identifiers that shouldn’t have been there. When she asked questions, her team dodged. When she pressed harder, Ava said quietly, “Don’t go chasing fires that aren’t yours to put out.”

Laneshia wanted to obey.
That was how you survived here. By choosing which truths to ignore.

But something about it kept scratching at her spirit.

That Sunday she went walking instead of going to church. The city was quiet. Early morning light cutting gold across the pavement. She passed the same mural she’d seen years ago, **pink roses breaking through concrete**. Someone had touched it up since then. The name *LAADIE OHH* still arched beneath it in bright white letters.

She stopped and just stared.

The memory rose in her like a song. The first time she'd seen it, how it had made her whisper "*still growing.*"

She took a photo on her phone. For reasons she couldn't name, she set it as her screensaver.

That week at work, she brought her concerns to a compliance officer. Quietly, carefully, and without drama. It was meant to be a small act of conscience, but in corporate ecosystems, small acts ripple big.

Within days, she was labeled *difficult*.
Meetings she once led were reassigned.
Ava stopped looping her in.

At first, Laneshia was furious. Then she was afraid. Then she was oddly… calm.

Because somewhere deep down, she knew she'd done the right thing. And that knowing, that quiet integrity, felt almost like faith again.

Two weeks later, HR called her in.

Ava sat across the table, unreadable. "We're restructuring," she said. "It's not personal."

Laneshia nodded. She'd rehearsed this moment in her head. "Of course," she said, voice steady.

They offered a generous severance. She took it. Walked out with a single box of belongings…. some books, her mug, a few notebooks.

Outside, the air felt thick and bright. For the first time in years, she wasn't rushing anywhere.

She stood on the sidewalk, watching traffic, her reflection ghosted in the glass doors of the building. Behind her, DynaCore kept humming with emails, deliverables, and progress. Ahead of her, an open horizon she hadn't expected.

She whispered, half-laughing, half-crying, "Well, God… I guess we're back here again."

In the weeks that followed, she slept. Read. Walked. She didn't rush to rebrand her unemployment as a "sabbatical." She let herself rest, really rest, for the first time in years.

Jamal called when he heard. "You okay?"

"I think so," she said. "It's strange. I lost something, but it doesn't feel like loss."

"That's 'cause you didn't lose yourself this time."

His words settled deep.

Slowly, creativity began creeping back into her days. She started volunteering with Jamal's art collective again, just on weekends at first. The first time she dipped a brush into color, she felt a shiver of recognition.

The paint was still there. The tenderness, too.

One afternoon she painted a small piece. A rose cracking through a gray wall. At the base, in tiny cursive, she wrote:

still growing

When the girls asked what it meant, she smiled.
"It means we don't have to stay who we were," she said. "Even if we forget for a while."

That night she opened her old journal and wrote:

Faith used to be obedience.
Then it became ambition.
Now I think it's just the courage to tell the truth and start again.

She closed the notebook, turned off the light, and slept dreamlessly.

Chapter Six ~ The Quiet Rebellion

2015.

The world had shifted again. Phones had become altars. Stories were currency. Everyone was branding themselves, performing meaning in bite-sized captions.

Laneshia had no interest in keeping up. But somehow, people kept finding her.

It started with a single photo. Her mural of the rose breaking through concrete, reposted by one of Jamal's students. The caption read:

"She says healing don't have to be pretty to be real."

By the end of the week, it had thousands of likes.
By the end of the month, she was getting messages from women across the country.

They wanted to know what her words meant.
They wanted to share their own stories. Of church girls who left, who lost, who learned how to live without permission.

Laneshia didn't plan to become anyone's voice. She just started posting small reflections. Bits of journal entries… fragments of prayer turned poetry.

Some of us ain't backsliding, she wrote one morning.
We just took the long way home to God.

That one went viral.

Suddenly, she was being invited to speak at women's gatherings, art exhibits, and faith podcasts. Her inbox overflowed. She laughed at the irony. How she'd spent years running from pulpits, only to end up building her own without meaning to.

Jamal teased her about it.

“You went from corporate rebel to spiritual influencer,” he said, grinning over dinner one night.

“I’m not an influencer,” she protested. “I’m just… talking.”

He raised an eyebrow. “You’re influencing people though.”

She rolled her eyes, but she knew he was right. The difference was that now her voice came from truth, not performance.

She called her platform *“The Quiet Rebellion.”*
It wasn’t about rage. It was about *reclaiming softness as strength.*

In her small apartment, things were different now. It was warmer, filled with plants and the scent of shea butter and sage. She built a rhythm again. Mornings were for writing. Afternoons for painting. Evenings for reflection or laughter with friends.

Her favorite ritual was stillness. She’d light a candle, sit cross-legged on the floor, and just breathe.

No sermons. No striving. Just silence, like a form of prayer.

Sometimes she thought of her mother. Ruth Ann was older now, softer around the edges but still bound to her church’s traditions. They spoke occasionally, careful and polite.

One afternoon, Ruth Ann called and said quietly, “I saw your video. About… healing. The one with the roses.”

Laneshia froze. “You did?”

“I don’t agree with everything you say,” her mother said slowly. “But… I understand some of it now.”

For the first time in decades, Laneshia heard something in her mother’s voice she’d never expected. Respect.

Chapter Seven ~ The Quiet Rebuilding

Healing didn't arrive with a trumpet or a grand revelation. It came slowly, like the first drops of rain on dry soil. Tentative, uneven, sometimes painful, and often unnoticed until the ground had already softened.

Laneshia did not plan to go to therapy. She had spent so many years trying to survive that vulnerability felt like a luxury she could not afford. But her company had partnered with a mental health service offering confidential counseling sessions, and after a night of restless sleep filled with fragments of dreams she could not remember but could not shake, she picked up the phone.

Her therapist, **Dr. Amina Holt**, was a Black woman in her fifties with eyes that seemed to see without judgment and a voice that drew Laneshia into honesty. Their first session was tentative. Laneshia spoke in circles. She bounced from the stress of work to her insomnia, and vague references to feeling "stuck." Dr. Holt listened, nodded, and occasionally asked a question that felt simple but cut straight to the heart: *What do you fear the most right now?*

Laneshia flinched at first. No one had asked her that before — not Malcolm, not her mother, not even her closest friends. But as the weeks passed, the walls she had built began to crack.

It wasn't easy.

Memories of her brother, of her mother's coldness, of Malcolm's subtle manipulations, emerged in therapy like stubborn weeds, tangled and resistant. She confronted them not all at once, but piece by piece, each session unraveling layers she had carried alone for decades.

One afternoon, after a particularly grueling session, Laneshia spoke the word she had carried like a stone in her throat for years:

"Molested," she whispered, almost afraid to breathe.

Dr. Holt's response was quiet, steady, and grounding. "That took courage to say out loud," she said. "You survived. And now, you're choosing to heal."

Laneshia realized in that moment that survival had not been enough. Surviving was passive. Healing required intention, effort, and the willingness to feel.

Therapy was only one thread in her rebuilding. She began journaling again, but not in the form of prayers. Instead, she wrote truths about pain, power, and about resilience. She documented her small victories at work, the friendships she nurtured, the moments when she stood up for herself without apology.

At work, Laneshia found empowerment in ways she had never imagined. She was promoted to lead a team on a software project, mentoring younger women who often faced the same doubts and insecurities she had experienced. She learned to speak up in meetings, to assert her opinions, and to navigate office politics with confidence.

At home, she began to create spaces that reflected who she wanted to be. Her apartment was filled with plants that thrived under her care, books she had long neglected, music that soothed rather than judged. She learned to delight in small pleasures. A perfectly brewed cup of coffee, a quiet evening spent coding, the rhythm of her own heartbeat.

Faith, however, remained complicated. Laneshia returned occasionally to church. Not the one she had grown up in, but a small, welcoming congregation that met in a rented auditorium. Here, faith was about honesty, not perfection. She began to understand that doubt did not make her a failure, and that questioning God was not betrayal.

Faith isn't about answers. It's about persistence. About showing up even when you don't understand why.

She clung to that thought as she navigated both her career and her personal life. She met other women. Survivors, professionals, mothers, and daughters. All who were also learning to exist fully in a world that had once tried to shrink them. Their stories became mirrors of her own. Affirming that she was not alone, and that her experiences, as painful as they were, could be transformed into guidance for others.

The rebuilding was not linear. There were setbacks. Nights when she longed for Malcolm's hollow validation. Mornings when childhood memories surged unbidden. Weeks when she questioned whether the effort to heal was even worth it. But each time, she returned to her tools. Therapy, journaling, work, and her emerging faith in herself.

By the time she turned forty-two, Laneshia realized something profound. She could survive without apology, exist without approval, and love herself without fear. She had learned that healing did not erase the past. It merely gave her the power to decide how she would carry it forward.

Intermission ~ What Remains

By forty-five, Laneshia Jonelle Stanson had stopped running from her own name.

Her mornings began quietly now, with rituals that grounded her in the present. Coffee brewed in a French press. Jazz hummed softly through the apartment. Sunlight streamed across the countertops, and she would pause to breathe deeply before the day began. For years, she had chased freedom and success, always with one foot in the past. But now, she walked forward fully. Aware of the weight she had shed and the resilience she had gained.

Her career had evolved alongside her. Laneshia had carved a niche in the tech industry. Not only as a developer and project lead, but also as a mentor for women entering a world that often undervalued them. The company had partnered with initiatives supporting diversity and leadership for women, and Laneshia volunteered to lead a mentorship circle. Once a month, she met with a small group of women in a glass-walled conference room, sharing sandwiches and coffee while speaking about the parts of life that didn't appear on spreadsheets: fear, doubt, ambition, and self-worth.

Sometimes the women cried. Sometimes Laneshia did too.

But every session reminded her that survival was only the first step; sharing her story was a form of purpose.

Then one Friday evening, her phone buzzed with a message that made her pause.

Malcolm J.: *Heard you're doing big things. Proud of you. Been thinking about you lately.*

Her heart tightened, not with longing, but with recognition. The old ache. The almost-forgotten wounds resurfaced briefly. He had a way of showing up when the air was clearing, like a storm refusing to be ignored.

She stared at the message, then closed it. She picked up her journal and wrote one line:

Not everyone who helped break you deserves to see you healed.

Weeks later, she saw him, by chance, at a tech-and-faith networking event downtown. He was older now, softer around the edges, wearing the same easy smile that had once made her forget herself.

"Laneshia," he said, reaching for her hand. "It's been a long time."

She looked at him calmly, feeling the memories rise and fall like waves. She had carried the lessons of patience, self-love, and resilience long enough to know this moment would not derail her.

"You're right," she said, smiling politely. "It's been a long time."

And that was all. She walked away without looking back, feeling neither anger nor longing. Only peace.

Laneshia's mentorship work became a source of profound fulfillment. She guided women navigating similar paths, listening to stories of struggle, survival, and quiet triumph. She helped them find the courage to set boundaries, to demand respect, and to trust themselves.

Her words, shaped by years of endurance, were simple but potent:

"Your story doesn't disqualify you. It's proof that you survived. And survival is sacred."

Through these interactions, Laneshia discovered a new dimension of faith. One that did not rely on perfection, certainty, or the validation of others. Faith was now a living, evolving conversation, rooted in self-awareness, empathy, and resilience.

She continued writing essays, blogs, and conference speeches sharing her journey honestly. Letters arrived from women all over the country. Pastors' daughters, survivors, and professionals. Women who had walked away from churches and communities that had once defined them. Their words reminded Laneshia that her life had meaning beyond survival: it had impact.

One night, she returned “home.” To the pine-scented roads of her childhood, carrying nothing but gratitude and memory. She parked where the old Stanson house had once stood. It was gone, replaced by a neat, modern home. She stood on the shoulder of the road and listened to the cicadas… feeling the same weight of heat and silence she had once feared. But this time, the heat warmed her. The silence embraced her.

There was no epiphany, no magical forgiveness, no sudden absolution. Only the quiet certainty that she had endured and endurance was strength.

That evening, she sat alone in her apartment, journal open, pen poised. She wrote:

I survived. I became. I forgive myself for needing time to heal.

And she spoke her own name aloud:

“Laneshia Jonelle Stanson.”

Not broken.
Not diminished.
Fully herself.

The cicadas hummed outside, and somewhere deep within her, she felt a light she had never known. Steady. Patient. Enduring.

For the first time, she understood: her faith, her purpose, and her love for life did not come from perfection, church, or approval. They came from herself.

And that was enough.

Months passed. Her audience grew. Publishers started calling. She signed a small book deal for a collection of essays and poems about womanhood, spirituality, and the messy middle between faith and freedom.

The title came to her in a dream:
"Church Girl Lost."

When she told Jamal, he just smiled. "You sure you ready for people to read your truth like that?"

She thought about it. "No," she said. "But I'm ready to stop hiding it."

The book came out the following year, modestly at first, then explosively. Women wrote to her from everywhere. Dallas, Detroit, Nairobi, even London! All expressing how they'd seen themselves in her pages.

Some said it gave them permission to question. Others said it helped them pray again.

She read their messages at night and cried quietly, the kind of tears that weren't about sadness or joy but release.

She realized that faith had never really left her. It had just changed dialects.

Still, not everything was easy. The more visible she became, the more people tried to box her in again. Some called her "the woman who left God." Others called her "the woman who made Him relevant again."

She learned to stop correcting them.
Her truth wasn't up for definition anymore.

One evening, at a panel event in Atlanta, someone asked:
"Do you still consider yourself a believer?"

Laneshia smiled. "I believe in grace," she said. "And I believe grace has many names."

The room went quiet. The kind of quiet that meant people were listening.

Afterward, she walked out into the cool night air. The mural of *LAADIE OHH* was still there, faded but undefeated. She ran her fingers over the paint again and whispered, like a ritual, “Still growing.”

Behind her, the city pulsed—sirens, laughter, gospel spilling from a passing car.

Ahead of her, the future felt open, not empty.

Fame didn’t arrive like thunder. It crept in quietly, then took up space.

At first, it was flattering. Speaking invitations, photo shoots, women lining up to hug her after readings. Then came the interviews, the endless questions from journalists who wanted her story to fit into something tidy.

“From preacher’s daughter to faith renegade.”
“From church pew to cultural prophet.”

They loved the contrast, the redemption arc.
They never wanted the middle. The lonely nights, the doubt, the grief of growing.

Laneshia smiled politely through it all, but sometimes after a panel she’d go home and sit in the dark, unsure if she was becoming a message instead of a person again.

Jamal was the one who kept her grounded.
He never called her *Church Girl Lost* or quoted her words back to her.
When they met, it was just life. Food, laughter and quietness.

They never made it official, never moved in together, but their bond deepened through years of small constancy.

One evening, while she was cooking, he said, “You know, you don’t owe anybody your transparency.”

She paused, spoon midair. “What do you mean?”

“Everybody keeps asking you to tell your story. But some parts are yours. They don’t need to be content.”

She thought about that for days.
How easily truth could become performance.
How even honesty could be commodified.

When her second book came out, *The Gospel of Softness*, it was more introspective. Slower. Some fans called it “too quiet.” But she didn’t care. It wasn’t written for applause. It was written for survival.

It opened with a letter to her younger self:

You don’t have to prove your goodness by breaking yourself open for others to watch you bleed. Healing can be private. Holiness can be quiet.

That line went viral, of course.
People tattooed it. Quoted it.
But for Laneshia, it wasn’t branding. It was confession.

Then came the invitation that shifted everything. A televised roundtable on faith and modern womanhood, hosted by one of the biggest networks in the South.

Her publicist was thrilled. “This is it, L. National audience. You could be the next Iyanla.”

Laneshia hesitated. She remembered the pulpits of her youth, the way visibility had always come with invisible cages.

Still, she agreed.

The night of the broadcast, she wore a simple white dress and no jewelry. Across from her sat a bishop, a pastor, and a lifestyle influencer. The conversation began civil. There was talk of balance, self-worth, and faith.

Then the bishop leaned in. “Miss Taylor, don’t you worry that your message leads people *away* from the church?”

Laneshia looked straight at him. “I think maybe we’ve confused the church with God.”

The room went silent. The host tried to smooth it over, but the moment lived. Raw and electric.

By morning, social media had divided itself again: half praising her courage, half calling her dangerous.

But Laneshia didn’t read the comments. She turned off her phone, went to the mural, and stood before it in the early light.

The pink roses had faded even more. The name *LAADIE OHH* was chipped, almost gone.

She smiled. “Everything changes,” she whispered. “Even what saves you.”

After that, she took a break from public life.
No announcements, no grand exits. Just space.

She spent her mornings walking through the city, afternoons painting, nights journaling. Sometimes she met up with Jamal; sometimes she didn’t. Silence had become her truest companion.

She started mentoring young women again. Not through organizations or branded platforms, but quietly, one on one.

When one of them asked how she knew when she’d “found herself,” Laneshia laughed softly.

“You don’t find yourself,” she said. “You return to yourself. Over and over again.”

That winter, she visited her mother for Christmas for the first time in years. The house smelled the same. Fried chicken, lemon polish, and faith lingering in the air.

Ruth Ann had aged, but her eyes were clear. After dinner, they sat together, and her mother said, “You were right about something.”

Laneshia blinked. “About what?”

“That God ain’t finished with any of us. I was so busy guarding His name, I forgot He don’t need guarding.”

Tears filled Laneshia’s eyes. “Mama—”

Ruth Ann squeezed her hand. “You turned out good, baby. Maybe not how I expected, but still good.”

It was the benediction she hadn’t known she’d been waiting for.

When she returned home, she opened her notebook again. The first page she wrote in months held just one sentence:

Maybe the quiet rebellion was never against the church.
Maybe it was against my own fear of being loved as I am.

She closed the journal, set it beside her bed, and looked out the window at the sleeping city.

For the first time in a long while, she didn't feel lost.
She just felt alive.

Chapter Eight~ The Book of Laneshia

By fifty-one, Laneshia Jonelle Stanson had stopped keeping track of time in years. She counted in seasons now. She counted them in projects completed, letters answered, women mentored, and mornings that began in peace.

Her apartment in midtown Atlanta was nothing grand, but sunlight loved it. It spilled across the hardwood floors in long, deliberate strokes, warming her coffee table, her books, and her laptop. Her plants leaned toward the light as if in prayer. She tended to them the way her grandmother had once tended to her. With care, patience, and quiet conversation.

"Grow how you need to," she'd whisper, misting their leaves. "Ain't no rush."

The city outside her window had changed again. The skyline higher. The streets, more crowded. But the heartbeat of Atlanta, that thrum of ambition and art and holy chaos, still called to her.

Laneshia now ran **The Rebuild Project**, a mentorship and scholarship initiative for women leaving faith-based trauma and rebuilding their lives in technology and leadership. The work was steady and soul deep. Each week, she sat in circles of women, laptops open, hearts trembling. Some were fresh out of marriages that had silenced them. Some were pastors' daughters still learning to name their pain. Some had never been to church at all but understood what it meant to worship something that didn't love you back.

Laneshia didn't preach. She listened.
She believed listening was its own kind of prayer.

When a woman cried too hard to speak, Laneshia would slide a tissue across the table and say softly, "You don't have to tell it all today. Just start with what hurts."

She never promised healing. Only direction.
Because she'd learned the truth the hard way. Healing wasn't a miracle. It was a discipline.

Her days followed a rhythm that suited her.
Morning walks through Piedmont Park.
Emails and funding proposals by mid-morning.
Mentorship calls after lunch.
Writing, always writing, in the evenings.

Her essays had matured. Less memoir and more reflection. They were tender letters to the living. Full of small lessons about grace, resilience, and the quiet art of staying.

Her latest collection, *The Weight of Light*, had just been shortlisted for a literary award. Her agent called to celebrate, but Laneshia simply smiled. "That's beautiful," she said. "But the real win is that it helped somebody feel seen."

She meant it. Fame had stopped seducing her long ago. What mattered now were the women who emailed her after reading her words:

"You helped me leave."
"You helped me forgive my mother."
"You reminded me that God still hears me, even when I can't pray."

Those were her awards.

Still, on quiet nights, she sometimes felt a subtle ache.
Not regret. Not loneliness exactly. Something else

A question that hummed beneath the surface of her calm:
What now, after survival? What comes after being whole?

It was the same question she avoided when she looked in the mirror and saw the softening lines around her mouth, the silver threading through her hair.

Sometimes she caught herself longing for the chaos. The hunger, the fight, the sharpness of old ambition.
Other times, she simply missed being *new*.

But each morning, she reminded herself: stillness was not stagnation. Growth didn't always roar.

That autumn, she received an email that made her pause.

Subject: Need Guidance — Urgent

Dear Ms. Stanson,
I'm writing because I don't know who else to talk to. I'm part of a church that's been my home since I was a child, but something's happening that doesn't feel right. They keep telling me to stay silent, to "let God handle it." I've seen your talks about reclaiming faith, and I think I need help.

— N.

The message didn't say much, but Laneshia felt it in her bones — the echo of a silence she had once known too well.

She replied immediately:

Hi N.,
You don't have to handle this alone. Let's talk.

She didn't know it then, but that single reply would become the hinge between the life she'd built and the next chapter of her becoming.

That week, she met Nia Daniels for coffee — a twenty-two-year-old college student with nervous eyes and trembling hands.

Nia reminded Laneshia of herself. The same church-trained politeness. The same quiet voice that carried the weight of too many expectations.

They sat by the café window as the city moved around them.
When Nia began to speak, her words came out halting, then urgent.

It wasn't a confession of sin, but of confusion. Of betrayal by a spiritual leader. Of being told that doubt was rebellion. Of being silenced in the name of submission.

Laneshia didn't flinch. She simply listened, nodding slowly, grounding the young woman in calm.

When Nia finished, her eyes filled with tears. "I thought maybe I was the problem," she whispered.

Laneshia reached across the table, her voice steady and warm.
"You're not the problem," she said. "You're the story."

Nia blinked. "What do you mean?"

"I mean your voice is the evidence that you're still here. That's where healing starts. When you stop whispering."

Nia exhaled, trembling. "I don't even know if I believe in God anymore."

Laneshia smiled gently. “Then start by believing in you. God can handle the rest.”

It was the same thing she’d once needed someone to tell her.

That night, after Nia left, Laneshia sat at her desk, the city glowing through her window. She opened her journal, its pages half-filled with drafts and prayers, and wrote:

I used to think my story ended when I found peace. But maybe peace isn’t the end. Maybe it’s the space where new faith begins.

She looked around her apartment, at the plants swaying gently in the lamplight, at the photos of women she’d helped, at her own reflection in the glass.

She didn’t feel lost.
She felt ready.

Ready for whatever the next chapter would ask of her.

Winter came softly that year.
Atlanta's skies turned the color of pewter, and the city slowed. The days were short, the air cold and forgiving.

Laneshia spent more time at home — teaching workshops online, writing between calls, watching the steam rise from her tea. She liked the stillness.

But Nia kept her busy, too.
They met weekly now. Not just for advice, but for what felt like spiritual re-parenting.

Nia was learning to rebuild her faith outside of obedience.
Laneshia was learning how to guide without rescuing.

One evening, after a particularly heavy talk, Nia said, "You always seem so certain. Like you've made peace with everything."

Laneshia smiled, shaking her head. "Certainty isn't peace, baby. It's just louder."

Nia frowned, processing that.
Laneshia continued, "Peace comes when you stop needing everything to make sense. That's when you start trusting life again."

Weeks passed.

Then, one night in February, Laneshia's phone rang after midnight.

It was her mother's neighbor, Mrs. Bailey. Her voice was soft but urgent.
"Baby, your mama's in the hospital. Nothing too bad yet, they just want to run tests. You might wanna come on down, though."

The world stilled.

By morning, Laneshia was on I-75 South, driving back toward the red clay and pine trees that had once been both her cradle and her cage.

The drive felt dreamlike. The sky a washed-out blue, gospel radio humming low. Each mile closer to home pulled her through layers of memory. The smell of fried catfish on Fridays, the sound of choir practice leaking through cracked windows, the ache of wanting to leave and the guilt of finally doing it.

When she reached the hospital, Ruth Ann was sitting up in bed, her Bible open, her hair wrapped neatly in a scarf.
“Girl, you came all this way for nothin’,” she said, smiling faintly. “Just a little scare.”

Laneshia laughed softly. “You and your scares.”

“I’m fine,” Ruth Ann insisted. “The Lord ain’t done with me yet.”

Laneshia sat beside her, holding her mother’s hand, noticing how the skin felt thinner now. Like delicate paper that time had written on.

They talked for hours. About the past. About the church. About life.
It wasn’t confessional, just honest.

At one point, Ruth Ann looked at her daughter and said, “You ever miss it? The old ways?”

Laneshia thought for a long moment.

“I miss the music,” she said. “The sound of people believing together. But I don’t miss being afraid to ask questions.”

Ruth Ann nodded. “You always did ask the hard ones.”

Before leaving town, Laneshia visited the old neighborhood.
The church still stood. Smaller than she remembered and its paint had faded. But across the street, the mural was gone.

Where *LAADIE OHH* once bloomed through concrete, there was now a parking lot. Only a faint trace of pink lingered on the corner of the curb, like a ghost of defiance.

Laneshia crouched and touched the concrete.
"It's all right," she whispered. "You bloomed long enough to remind me how."

She stayed there a while, wind lifting her scarf, the sound of cars passing like hymns without words.

That night, she stayed in her mother's house. The one she'd once run from.
She sat at the kitchen table with her notebook, the same way she had as a girl, listening to the quiet hum of the refrigerator.

Her pen moved slowly.

The church taught me to confess, but life taught me to testify.
Confession says: I was wrong.
Testimony says: I survived.

She wrote until the page was full, then closed the notebook and let her head rest on her arms.

Outside, the moonlight poured through the window like grace.

In the morning, she and Ruth Ann sat on the porch with coffee.
Birds sang from the pecan tree. The world felt clean.

Ruth Ann said, "You know, I been thinkin'.... maybe God don't live in churches no more. Maybe He moved into people."

Laneshia smiled. “Maybe He always did.”

They laughed softly together.

Later that spring, back in Atlanta, Nia called with good news. She’d been accepted into a graduate program for counseling.

“I couldn’t have done it without you,” Nia said.

“Yes, you could have,” Laneshia replied. “You just needed someone to remind you that your voice was already waiting.”

After they hung up, Laneshia stood by the window, sunlight breaking through the clouds.

Her reflection in the glass looked both older and freer. A woman made of faith, doubt, and survival in equal measure.

She whispered to her own reflection, “Church girl found.”

And for the first time, the words didn’t sound like a declaration.
They sounded like peace.

That night, she began writing her final book.
Not memoir, not theology, but something else.

It began:

There are women who were told they were too loud, too curious, too much like God Himself. Wild, creative, and uncontainable. This is their gospel. This is mine.

The title came easily, as if it had been waiting all along:
The Book of Laneshia.

Epilogue ~ The Rose and the Name

Years later, after the world had shifted yet again, people still quoted Laneshia Stanson.
They called her *the woman who wrote God in lowercase,* the one who turned her silence into scripture.

But the people who knew her, like really knew her, said she was something simpler. A mirror. A woman who taught you to see yourself clearly, even when the light was dim.

After her passing, *The Rebuild Project* continued under Nia's direction. They renamed the main studio *The LAADIE Room* after the word that had first bloomed in paint and concrete. That symbol of softness growing out of hard things.

The new mural stood just outside the entrance.
A single pink rose, petals vivid against the wall.
Beneath it, the words curved in a crescent:

LAADIE OHH ~ We Still Bloom.

People came from all over to see it. Not tourists, but seekers. Women with stories in their throats. Men carrying apologies. Children learning that holiness could look like laughter.

No one really knew who first painted the rose that inspired it.
Some said it had appeared overnight back in the early 2000s, after a heavy rain, like the earth itself had decided to speak.

But those who had known Laneshia understood.
They'd seen how she could turn broken ground into a garden.

One spring morning, years after her death, Nia visited the mural alone. The city was waking. Sirens in the distance, pigeons scattering, the scent of honeysuckle mixing with exhaust.

She placed a single fresh rose at the foot of the wall and whispered, "Thank you."

And for just a moment, maybe it was wind, maybe imagination, she thought she heard Laneshia's voice, low and warm, say:

"Still growing."

The petals trembled.
The light shifted.
And the concrete beneath her feet felt soft —
as if the world itself remembered.

The Rose in the Concrete

by Laadie Ohh

I once knelt beneath the weight of my worry,
Crying out to Heaven through cracks in my soul.
Every why I whispered felt unanswered and hollow,
And faith seemed a dream I could no longer hold.
But even in silence, His mercy was speaking
In every bruise, a blessing unseen was growing.

I had to break to learn I was built for beauty,
To see God's grace bloom in the dirt and despair.
He took the ashes I wore as armor,
And wove them to crown my courage with care.
In the rubble, I heard Him remind me softly:
"My daughter, you were never broken…only becoming."

Now I rise with purpose, petals wide open,
A rose in the concrete, kissed by the Son.

Each scar a scripture, each tear a testimony

Proof that faith's fight is never truly done.

To every woman still wandering through the wilderness:

Keep going, beloved, your growth has just begun.

~ Laadie Ohh ~

Acknowledgements

*First and foremost, I thank **God** for the grace that covered me even when I couldn't see it, and for never letting my story end in the middle of the storm. Every word in these pages is a testimony that healing is possible, even for the ones who thought they were too broken to begin again.*

To every woman who has ever questioned her worth, her faith, or her reflection in the mirror, this book is for you. May it remind you that even the lost can be found, and even the shattered can shine again.

To my family and loved ones, thank you for standing with me as I poured my heart into this story. Your patience, love, and belief in me carried me through every late night and every tear-stained page.

To my sisters in faith and every soul who shared their truth with me. Your courage lit a fire in mine. You taught me that testimony isn't about perfection; it's about survival, surrender, and grace.

To the readers, thank you for taking this journey with Laneshia. I pray her story reaches the corners of your heart that need to be reminded that you are not alone.

And finally, to the little girl inside me who once felt unseen, I see you now. You made it.

With love,
Laadie Ohh

LAADIE OHH

Made in the USA
Coppell, TX
30 December 2025

67621246R00055